Sometimes it's hard being a goldfish. You dream of growing fat and exploring coral reefs. But instead here you are in a bowl. Going round and round in circles.

And sometimes it's hard being a child in the summer in the city. All your friends leave and there's no one to play with. You dream of escaping the steamy heat, too. But instead here you are in an apartment. Going round and round in circles.

But sometimes—

well, something

happens to change

all that. . . .

GoldFish.
ON
VACATION

WORDS BY
SALLY LLOYD-JONES

PICTURES BY
LEO ESPINOSA

schwartz & wade books · new york

In a small apartment, in a tall round building, by a park, next to a river, in the middle of the big city, there lived three children:

H,
Little O,
and Baby Em.

In a small bowl, next to a lamp, in the
middle of a table, beside the curtains, in the
small apartment, there lived three goldfish:
Barracuda,
Patch,
and Fiss.

An old fountain stood at the end of their street. It was broken
and covered in ivy. No one used it anymore—except to throw garbage in.
But the children thought it was beautiful.
On top of the fountain there perched—as if he'd just landed or was
just about to fly off—a magnificent stone eagle with outstretched wings.

Grandpa said the same people who built the famous Grand Central Station built the fountain. And in the Olden Days Before Cars, horses drank from it.

But when people got cars, they didn't need horses—or the fountain. And they stopped taking care of it.

The children felt sad for the fountain and the eagle.

Then one early summer day, a sign appeared:

The children rushed home to tell their fish.

"You're going on vacation!"

Barracuda stared with his big fish eyes.

Fiss blew big fiss bubbles.

And Patch sank slowly down to the bottom of the bowl.

"See!" H said. "They can't wait!"

Grandpa rushed into the kitchen. And on the big calendar
on the wall, next to June 28, he wrote: *Goldfish on vacation*

But the children didn't need a calendar to remember.
They were already counting the days. Every morning they
rushed to the window (and so did Grandpa). And every
morning they watched a man at the fountain.

One morning, he was cleaning.

The next morning, he was
scrubbing and scraping.

Another morning, he pulled ivy off the eagle and
filled the fountain with clear, cold water.

He put in tall reeds.
And then lily pads.

And then one morning, the children couldn't
see him. They couldn't see him because . . .

because of all the children! The children and children
and children crowding around him! All of them waiting
to drop off their little fish children.

"It's TODAY!" cheered H, Little O, and Baby Em.
And it was.

In no time they were making their way slowly down the big staircase and out the front door: Grandpa leading the way, then Little O with her net, then Baby Em with the fish food, then H with the bowl and Barracuda and Patch and Fiss—in a wonderful Goldfish Parade.

Out on the street, everywhere they looked, there were goldfish parents just like them, with their goldfish.

When at last it was their turn at the fountain,
H and Baby Em and Little O told their fish goodbye
and see you soon and don't be homesick.

Then the man helped them lower the bowl underwater. At first the fish hung back in the bowl, until—in a flash of light, they darted and were gone.

The water shone in the shadow of the eagle's wings.
And the children saw, glistening in the sunlight,
swimming in the clear, cool pool—like sudden glimpses
of hidden treasure—fish after golden fish.

All through the hot summer, H, Little O, and Baby Em stopped by to say hello to their goldfish. And so did the other goldfish parents.

Soon all the children looked forward to meeting each other at the fountain. Every day they played together. And every day Grandpa came and put his chair down and chatted with the children, who sat and listened.

And he told them stories of those hot August days long ago when he was a boy, and how all the children who couldn't leave the city would jump and splash in the fountain.

And then the children wished that they were those children jumping in.

Before they knew it, it was the end of the summer.

The man told the goldfish parents that the only way to catch their fish was to go in the fountain. To wade into the water with their nets.

And so all the children took off their sandals and jumped and splashed and laughed in the fountain.

And then Grandpa took off his sandals, too—and rolled up his trousers and paddled. And he said it was like those days long ago, when he was a boy.

And the children could hardly even recognize their goldfish—they looked like completely different fish. "Are they really OUR fish?" asked Little O as they headed home.

"Oh, yes, I'm absolutely certain they're our fish!" said Grandpa, who really wasn't at all certain they were.

"They look so fat and happy," said H.

"Of course!" said Grandpa. "That's what a vacation will do for you. Anyway, who says you have to leave the city to have a vacation?"

And the children laughed because they knew it was true.

And so the goldfish—who may have been
Barracuda and Patch and Fiss, or some other goldfish
altogether—went back to being fish in a bowl.

And the children went back to being children in school. Until the next summer, when Hamilton Fountain would once again be filled with lily pads and reeds and shining water and golden fish.

And children.

For H, Little O, and Baby M —S.L.J.

For my parents, Mariantonia and Ernesto —L.E.

Author's Note

This is a true story that happened in New York City over the summers of 1992 to 2005.

The fountain is on Riverside Drive and 76th Street. It is called Hamilton Fountain, after Robert Ray Hamilton (1851–1890), who gave it to New York. (Actually, he was the great-grandson of a very famous Hamilton—Alexander Hamilton, a founding father of the United States.)

The man who came to clean the fountain was called Brad, a volunteer with the Riverside Park Conservancy.

The tall round building is famous because the artist Marc Chagall lived there for about ten years in the 1940s. He loved it for the wonderful light.

The three children and their goldfish and their grandpa were inspired by my nieces and nephews and their goldfish and granddad—but I made it up about them living in New York. They all live in England. (I didn't make up any of the other bits, though. I promise.)

So you see, it's a completely true made-up story.

In 2009, someone gave money for the fountain to be restored. And at last, it was.

Text copyright © 2017 by Sally Lloyd-Jones

Jacket art and interior illustrations copyright © 2017 by Leo Espinosa

All rights reserved. Published in the United States by Schwartz & Wade Books, an imprint of Random House Children's Books, a division of Penguin Random House LLC, New York.

Schwartz & Wade Books and the colophon are trademarks of Penguin Random House LLC.

Visit us on the Web! randomhousekids.com

Educators and librarians, for a variety of teaching tools, visit us at RHTeachersLibrarians.com

Library of Congress Cataloging-in-Publication Data is available upon request.

ISBN 978-0-385-38611-1 (hc)

ISBN 978-0-385-38612-8 (lib. bdg.)

ISBN 978-0-385-38613-5 (ebook)

The text of this book is set in 17-point Filosofia.

The illustrations were rendered in pencil and Adobe Photoshop.

MANUFACTURED IN CHINA

10 9 8 7 6 5 4 3 2 1

First Edition

Random House Children's Books supports the First Amendment and celebrates the right to read.

NO GOLDFISH WERE HARMED DURING THE MAKING OF THIS BOOK. STORY WRITTEN ENTIRELY ON LOCATION.